빗 방 울

이 정 자

국학자료원

A raindrop

Lee Jeongja

Sijo translation study meeting

國學資料院

KookHak

역자의 말

우연한 기회에 어떤 계기로 2009년부터 영역시조에 관심을 갖고 서서히 번역한 것이 고시조부터 현대시조에 이르기까지 수 백여 편에 이른다. 물론 [한국시조문학] 1호부터 제7호까지 발표한 150여 편과 [한국문학신문] 에 2011년부터 발표된 작품 80여 편도 포함된다. '구슬이 서말이라도 꿰어야 보배'라는 속언이 있듯이 이 중에서 1인 1편씩 1차로 75편을 선하여 출간하기로 한다. 곧 75명 시조시인의 영역작품이 한 권으로 소개된다.

본 시조 번역은 한국어와 영어의 음수율을 맞추어 번역하였다. 예를 들면 '언제나'를 번역하는데 'always' 이면 영어로는 2음절이다. 우리말의 3음절을 맞추기 위해 'all the time'으로 했다. 이렇게 의미가 같으면서 음절까지 같게 번역하였다. 일반적으로 이렇게 음절까지 맞추어 번역을 하지 않음을 보게 된다. 이는 시조를 자유시 같이 쓰는 것과 같다고 할 수 있다. 이에 필자는 시조를 정격으로 쓰듯이 번역도 정격에 맞추어 하려고 한다. 그래야만 제대로의 시조의 맛을 외국인에게 느끼게 하기 위해서이다. 물론

그래야만 시조의 정체성을 제대로 전할 수 있기 때문이다. 필자(역자)의 이러한 견해는 임종찬·박향선 교수의 <시조의 외국어역 문제 고찰-한역(漢譯)과 영역(英譯)을 중심으로>가 'FIT 2008 세계 대회'에서 발표한 것을 보면서 더욱 힘을 실어 주었다.

　예컨대 '이 몸이/죽어 가서(3·4)/무엇이/ 될꼬 하니(3·4)// 봉래산/제일봉에(3·4)/낙락장송/되었다가(4·4)//백설이/만건곤할 제(3·5)/독야청청/하리라(4·3)'라는 성삼문의 시조를 살펴보자.

　리차드 럿의 번역을 보자.

'When this frame/is dead and gone(3·4)/
what will then/become of me?(3·4)//
On the peak/of Pongnae-san/(3·4)
I shall become/a spreading pine(4·4)//
When white snow/fills heaven and earth(3·5)
I shall still stand/lone and green(4·3)'

이 번역은 한글 시조작품의 음절수와 영어 번역문의 음절수가 (초장)3 · 4/3 · 4//(중장)3 · 4/4 · 4//(종장)3 · 5/4 · 3 으로 정확히 일치한다.

반면 켈빈 오루크의 번역은 그렇지 않다.

'You asked me/what I'll be(3음절·3음절)/
when this body /is dead and gone?(4·4)//
On the topmost peak/of Pongnaesan(5·4)//
A great spreading pine/is what I'll become(5·5)//
There to stand/alone and green(3·4)/
when snow fills/all heaven and earth(3·5).

이 번역은 시조 원문이 허용하는 음수율을 위반함으로써 시조 본연의 형식을 해치고 있다.

같은 시조를 두고도 위에서 보듯이 번역에 차이가 있음을 본다. 이에 필자는 리차드 럿의 방법을 취한 것이다.

시조의 구 개념과 마찬가지로 번역도 음보 중심이 아니라 구 중심으로 함이 의미전달이 정확함을 알게 된다. 리차드 럿도 구 중심으로 번역했음을 알 수 있다.

시조의 의미 번역과 함께 외국인을 위한 한국어 독음을 돕기 위해서 로마자 독음을 병기 했다. 올해는 특히 국제 펜대회가 한국에서 열리는 해이다. 국제PEN한국본부에서는 한글문학 큰잔치인 세계한글작가대회를 9월 15일부터 18일까지 천년고도인 경주에서 개최한다. 세계한글작가대회는 한글의 우수성과 함께 한국문학을 전 세계에 알리는 좋은 계기가 될 것이다. 특히 우리 고유의 정형시인 시조를 전 세계에 알리는 좋은 기회가 될 것으로 기대한다. 그래서 그 시기에 맞추어 이정자의 영역시조(1)를 출판하기로 했다. 가장 한국적인 것이 세계적이라는 말을 새겨보면서-.

한글의 로마자 표기는 김홍렬 시인이 수고해 주었다. 김 시인은 "국어의 로마자 표기법(2000. 7. 7 문화관광부 고시 제2000-8호)"에 따라 서울 대 이상억 교수와 부산대 정보컴퓨터 공학부 <인공지능 연구실>과 (주) 나라 인포테크가 공동 개발한 시스템을 참고하였고, 인명, 행정구역, 학술용어, 일반(문장) 중 일반(문장)의 전환 방법을 원칙으로 삼았음을 밝힌다. 더불어 부록으로 로마자 표기법을 말미에 실었다.

아무쪼록 이정자의 영역시조(1)가 시조의 세계화를 향한 걸음에 일익을 담당하고 한 발 다가가는 데 보탬이 되기를 바란다.

2015. 7.

자헌 이정자

The Introduction

Sijo is poetry native to Korea. It is distinguished from free poems as a separate identity that it has its own formal beauty, and the works that deviate from this poetic rule are guarded against. In the past ancient Sijo, in terms of both music and literature, was a major genre in harmony with Chang(songs), however, in modern times, It has been created irrelevantly with Chang.

With most English-version Sijo works, foreign readers can't feel the specific character of Sijo works because it is not proper to translate Sijo works in accordance with the formality of English poetry.

For example, Following English translation of the best known Korean Sijo is Seong Sam Moon's 'Constant song'. Let's read the following Sijo together.

['You asked me/what I'll be(3·3)/
when this body /is dead and gone?(4·4)//
On the topmost peak/of Pongnaesan(5·4)//
A great spreading pine/is what I'll become(5·5)//
There to stand/alone and green(3·4)/
when snow fills/all heaven and earth(3·5).']
(translated by Calvin Olooke)

This is not in accord with Sijo's form, so I have been opposing to Calvin's translation. While the following does not; Let's compare, the two, the former with the latter.

['When this frame/is dead and gone(3·4)/
what will then/become of me?(3·4)//
On the peak/of Pongnae-san/(3·4)
I shall become/a spreading pine(4·4)//
When white snow/fills heaven and earth(3·5)
I shall still stand/lone and green(4·3)']
(translated by Richard Luts)]

This translation exactly agrees with Korean and English syllables in Sijo; first verse: 3/4/3/4, the middle verse: 3/4/4/4, the last verse:3/5/4/3.

I have been translating Sijo works in English by Richard Luts' method.

Lee Jeongja

순 서(contents)

제2부 : part2

제3부 : part3

제4부 : part4

제5부 : part5

제1부

빗방울 bi-ppang-ul

강만수 Kang Mansu

빗방울 하나가
bit-bang-ul ha-na-ga
강물에 떨어지고
gang-mu-re tteo-reo-ji-go

동그라미
dong-geu-ra-mi
하나 그리고
ha-na geu-ri-go
강물로 사라지고
gang-mul-ro sa-ra-ji-go

삶이란
sal-mi-ran
작은 동그라미
ja-geun dong-geu-ra-mi
강물에 그리는 것.
gang-mu-re geu-ri-neun geot.

여수 (yeo-su)

전 규 태(Jeon Gyutae)

상한 날개 다 나으면
sang-han nal-gae da na-eu-myeon
하늘 멀리 떠나고파
ha-neul meol-li tteo-na-go-pa

돌아올 기약 없는
dora-ol gi-ya-geom-neun
길손이고 싶어라
gil-son-i-go si-peo-ra

머잖을
meo-ja-neul
사랑 나누는
sar-ang na-nu-neun
세월이고 싶어라.
se-wo-ri-go si-peo-ra.

Melancholy on a journey

Jeon Gyutae

When my injured wing recovers,
I would like to leave the sky far.

Without a pledge to come back,
I'd like to be a traveller.

Not too far,
Making love each other,
I want to be all these years.

눈물 (nun-mul)

김 준(kim Jun)

지니고 싶은 것이
ji-ni-gosi-peun-geo-sie
어찌 웃음 뿐이랴만
eojjiu-sumppu-ni-rya-man

세월의 갈피마다
sewo-rui gal-pi-ma-da
어려움 쌓다보면
eo-ryeo-um ssa-tta-bo-myeon

눈물도 그것만큼의
nun-mul-do geu-geot-man-keu-mui
큰 의미를 지닌다.
keun ui-mi-reul ji-nin-da.

Tears

Kim Jun

That I am willing to have,
Why is it only laughing?
Every between the leaves of years,
Having in difficulties,
Tears also, bear a great meaning
So much as those possess.

빗방울 (bi-ppang-ul)

강 만 수(Kang Mansu)

빗방울 하나가
bi-ppang-ul ha-na-ga
강물에 떨어지고
gang-mu-re tteo-reo-ji-go

동그라미 dong-geu-ra-mi
하나 그리고 ha-na geu-ri-go
강물로 사라지고 gang-mul-ro sa-ra-ji-go

삶이란 sal-mi-ran
작은 동그라미 ja-geun dong-geu-ra-mi
강물에 그리는 것. gang-mu-re geu-ri-neun-geot

A raindrop

Kang Mansu

A raindrop
Falls in the river water,

It Draws a circle
And disappears into the river

The Life is
A little circle,
To draw a circle on the river.

억새꽃 (eok-sae-kkot)

리 강 룡(Lee Gangryong)

잎도 꽃도 이만해야
ip-do kko-tto I-man-hae-ya
붓 한 자루 맬 수 있다
bu-tan-ja-ru mael-su it-da

매몰찬 바람 앞에
mae-mol-chan ba-ram a-pe
목이 댕강 떨어져도
mo-gi daeng-gang tteo-leo-jyeo-do

제 소신 굽히지 않고
je so-sin gu-pi-ji an-ko
하얀 시를 남긴다.
ha-yan si-reul nam-gin-da.

The eulalia

Lee Gangryong

Leaves, flowers too, are done as these,
You can make a brush with them.

In front of the very cold wind,
As though their necks fall with clangs.

They do not bend their convictions,
And are left their white poetry.

예송리 전망대에서 (yesong-ri jeon-mang-dae-e-seo)

이 근 구(Lee Geungu)

숲 · 바다
sup ba-da
반달해변
ban-dal hae-byeon
무릉이 예로구나
mu-reung-i ye-ro-gu-na

고산도 자연빙하
go-san-do ja-yeon-bing-ha
무릎 치며 반겼으리
mu-reup chi-myeo ban-gyeo sseu-ri

촌부도
chon-bu-do
이쯤에서는
i-jjeu-me-seo-neun
시 한 수 안 읊으랴.
si han su an eul-pu-rya.

At the Yesong belvedere

Lee Geungu

The wood-sea,
A half moon beach,
Here is an Arcadia.

Gosan* too, in the naturel,
would be pleased beating his knees.

Chonbu* too,
In this Utopia,
How doesn't compose a poem.

* Gosan: Yunseondo's pseudonym
* Chonbu : Korean language, a country man

바름이의 미소 (bareumi-ui miso)

채 현 병(Chae Hyeonbyeong)

열 달을 채우고도
yeol da-reul chae-u-go-do
또 엿새 준비터니
tto yeot-ssae jun-bi-teo-ni
꿈속을 깨어나듯
kkum-so-geul kkae-yeo-na-deut
세상에 나왔어라
se-sang-e na-wa-sseo-ra
이삼일 지내보더니
i-sa-mil ji-nae-bo-deo-ni
미소부터 짓더라.
mi-so-bu-teo jit-deo-ra.

* 바름이 : 외손주 胎名

Bareume's smile

Chae Hyeonbyeong

Filling up ten months,
And adding to there six days.
As she wakes up inside a dream,
comes into the world.
In two or three days after birth,
The baby, Bareumi smiles.

* Bareume: a fetus name of the baby

쟁 취 (jaeng-chwi)

송 귀 영(Song Gwiyeong)

밤벌레 잔치 벌린
bam-beol-re jan-chi beol-rin
수액의 옹달샘에
su-ae-gui ong-dal-saem-e

육중한 사슴벌레
yuk-jung-han sa-seum beol-re
느닷없이 달려든다.
neu-dat-eop-si dal-ryeo-deun-da

숲속은 정글의 법칙
sup-sso-geun jeong-geu-lui beob-chik
전리품은 강자의 몫.
jeol-li-pum-eun gang-ja-ui mok.

A winner

Song Gwiyeong

At a spring of sap
That the night-worm has a feast,

Massive stag beetles
Rush at unexpectedly.

Woods is the law of the jungle.
Booty is a share of the strong.

두둠실 산내방을 짓다 · 7

(du-dum-sil san-nae-bang-eul jit-da)

정 정 조(Jeong Jeongjo)

미지생 미지시에
mi-ji-saeng mi-ji-si-e
양친을 멀리 보내
yang-chin-eul meol-li bo-nae

두 눈으론 못 뵈어도
du nu-neu-ron mot boe-eo-do
마음만은 지척인 것을
ma-eom-man-eun ji-cheo-gin geo-seul

응어리 번민한 한에
eung-eo-ri beon-min-han han-e
달집 한 채 바쳐 본다.
dal-jip han chae ba-chyeo bon-da.

Dudumsil sanraebang*

Jeong Jeongjo

Not knowing cause and result of it,
Sending my parents away.

Though I don't see them with two eyes,
They are always in my heart.

I offer my house with my heart
Them suffered a lot of grief.

Dudumsil sanraebang*

* Korean proper name, that is a room name.

푸르른 날에는 (pu-reu-reun na-re-neun)

정 수 자(Jeong Suja)

이자도 안 아까워 i-ja-do an a-kka-wo
우정 은행에 간다 u-jeong eun-haeng-e gan-da

무담보에 mu-dam-bo-e
무한량의 mu-hal-lyang-ui
금싸라기 geum-ssa-ra-gi
가을햇살 ga-eul haet-ssal

숨조차 sum-jo-cha
호사스러워 ho-sa-seu-reo-wo
삼가듯 sam-gi-deut
떨며 간다 tteol-myeo gan-da

On the green day

Jeong Suja

The interest, too does not grudge.
I go to the friendship bank.

Unsecured,
Infinite,
Gold dust*,
Autumn sun light,

Even breathe,
Too extravagant,
I go to there carefully.

*a thing of great value

봄꽃 (bom-kkot)

유 자 효(Yu Jahyo)

바람 불어 꽃이 지니
ba-ram bu-reo bom-kko-chi ji-ni
양산 위에 꽃이 피고
yang-san wi-e kko-chi pi-go

하늘하늘 걷는 자태
ha-neul-ha-neul geon-neun ja-tae
꽃보라 속 또 한 꽃
kkot-bo-ra sok tto han kkot

이 봄은 꽃들의 환호
i-bo-meun kkot-deu-rui hwan-ho
황홀해서 슬픈 꽃
hwang-hol-hae-seo seul-peun kkot

Spring flowers

Yu Jahyo

The wind blows, the flowers fall,
The flower blooms on the Parasol

Haneul haneul* walking figure,
The another flower among flowers,

This spring is the cheers of the flowers,
The sad flower in ecstasy.

* Haneul haneul : Koren mimetic word, to move softly.

관용의 인연 (gwan-yong-ui I-nyeon)

노 창 수(No Changsu)

괜찮아 gwan-cha-na
손 뒤집듯 son dui-jip-deut
터놓고 말하지 말라 teo-noko mal-ha-ji mal-ra

만암 선사 낙초자비 ma-nam seon-sa nak-cho-ja-bi
실천한 도량이었다. sil-cheon-han do-ryang-i-yeot-da

첫 세상 cheot se-sang
치솟은 산사 chi-so-seun san-sa
법문 스쳐 오른다. beom-mun seu-cheo o-reun-da.

Karma of generosity

No Changsu

Not so bad,
As you turn out your hands
Don't speak openly.

It was a broad minded practiced
Man-am Zen priest Nakchojaby,*

The first world,
Towering Buddhist temple,
I climb up the Buddhism.

* 낙초자비(落草慈悲) : to give fallen leaves a mercy. to bestow a
favor

님의 향기 (nim-ui hyang-gi)

오 병 두(Oh Byeongdu)

가슴 속 ga-seum ssok
묵향처럼 muk-hyang-cheo-reom
베어든 님의 향기 bae-eo-deun hyang-gi

진실을 토해 내는 jin-si-reul to-hae nae-neun
고뇌 속 맑은 내음 go-noe ssok mal-geun nae-eum

자욱한 ja-u-kan
행복 마루에 haeng-bok ma-ru-e
님의 자취 그린다. nim-ui ja-chwi geu-rin-da.

Lover's perfume

Oh Byeongdu

In my heart,
Like black ink scent
Impressed lover's perfume,

Crystal odor in agony expressing sincerity,

I draw on
The trace of my lover
On the floor in happiness.

글빛으로 (geul-bi-cheu-ro)

최 봉 희(Choi Bonghui)

소리빛 so-ri-bit
여울 따라 yeo-ul tta-ra
흐르는 글말살이 heu-reu-neun geul-mal-sa-ri

나랏말 na-rat-mal
고운 빛에go-un bi-che
올곧게 어울러서ol-got-ge eo-ul-reo-seo

온종일on jong-il
살을 맞대고sa-reul mat-dae-go
꽃잠 자듯 살겠네 kkot-jam ja-deut sal-gen-ne.

As letters

Choi Bonghui

Letters
Streaming according to
A current of the light of sound,

Joining with fine color
Of the word of state, upright,

The whole day,
They shall live on flesh to flesh
As if flower sleep does.

땅 (ttang)

이 승 현(Lee Seunghyeon)

무수한 생명을 mu-su-han saeng-myeong-eul
품었다 놓는 흙의 숨결 pu-meot-da non-neun sum-gyeol

그 바람 한 가운데 geu ba-ram han ga-un-de
어머니가 계셨다 eo-meo-ni-ga ge-syeot-da

광야는gwang-ya-neun
만물의 자궁man-mul-ui ja-gung
나를 낳고 키웠다na-reul na-ko ki-wot-da.

The ground

Lee Seung-hyeon

A breath of soil
That entertaining and putting
Countless life in its bosom,

There was existence Mother
In the middle of the wind.

A wide plain,
The womb of the creation,
Gave birth to me and raised.

봄비 (bom-bi)

이 정 자(Lee Jeong ja)

저리도 부드럽게
jeo-ri-do bu-deu-reop-ge
조심스레 세필 세워
jo-sim-seu-re se-pil se-wo

촉촉이 스며들어
chok-chok-i seu-myeo-deu-reo
여백을 채우면서
yeo-bae-geul chae-u-myeon-seo

대지에
dae-ji-e
풍경 그리는
pung-gyeong geu-ri-neun
조물주의 초록 꿈.
jo-mul-ju-ui cho-rok kkum

Spring rain

Lee Jeongja

In that way, carefully
Erecting a slender brush,

Soaking moderately wet,
Filling up the vacancy,

On the ground,
Drawing scenery,
It is the green dream of God.

제2부

반달 ban-dal

원용우 Won Yong-u

동행하던 내 짝이
dong-haeng-ha-deon nae jja-gi
하늘나라 가시었나
ha-neul-na-ra ga-si-eon-na
떨어져 나간 반쪽
tteo-leo-jyeo na-gan ban-jjok
너무 시린 등뼈가
neo-mu si-rin deung-bbyeo-ga
하얗게 그리움 뿜고
ha-ya-ke geu-ri-um bbum-go
허공중에 걸렸다.
heo-gong-jung-e geol-ryeot-da.

분이네 살구나무 (bun-i-ne sal-gu-na-mu)

정 완영(Jeong Wanyeong)

동네서 젤 작은집
dong-ne-seo jel ja-geun-jip
분이네 오막살이
bu-ni-ne o-mak-sal-ri
동네서 젤 큰 나무
dong-ne-seo jel keun na-mu
분이네 살구나무
bu-ni-ne sal-gu-na-mu
밤사이 활짝 펴올라
bam-sai hwal-jjak pyeo-ol-ra
대궐보다 덩그렇다.
dae-gwol-bo-da deong-geu-reot-ta.

The apricot tree of Buni family

Jeong Wanyeong

The least home in a village
Is the hut of Boni Family.
The largest tree in a village
Is the apricot tree of Buni family
It bursts into blossom in the night,
Is stately than the royal palace.

반달 (ban-dal)

원 용 우(Won Yong-u)

동행하던 내 짝이
dong-haeng-ha-deon nae jja-gi
하늘나라 가시었나
ha-neul-na-ra ga-si-eon-na
떨어져 나간 반쪽
tteo-leo-jyeo na-gan ban-jjok
너무 시린 등뼈가
neo-mu si-rin deung-bbyeo-ga
하얗게 그리움 뿜고
ha-ya-ke geu-ri-um bbum-go
허공중에 걸렸다.
heo-gong-jung-e geol-ryeot-da.

A half moon

Won Yong-u

Accompanied by me, my spouse,
Did she have gone to heaven?

The backbone too chilly of
My half, partner separated

Have blown off longing snow-white and
Have hung in the middle space.

서울역 지하도 (seoul-yeok ji-ha-do)

김 홍 열(Kim Heungryeol)

어딘가 한 번쯤은eo-din-ga han beon-jjeu-meun
제구실 했을 못이je-gu-sil hae-sseul mo-si
찬 바닥 여기저기chan ba-dak yeo-gi jeo-gi
흩어져서 나뒹군다.heu-teo-jeo na-duing-gun-da.

누군가nu-gun-ga
똑바로 펴면ttok-ba-ro pyeo-myeon
다시 쓸 수 있을 텐데.da-si sseul-su i-sseul ten-de.

The underpass of Seoul station

Kim Heung-yeol

Anywhere, by the time once,
Nails had done their duties,
Roll over scattering
On the cold ground here and there.

If someone
Might straighten these nails,
They could be used well again.

어머니 34 (eo-meo-ni 34)

신 웅 순(Sin Wungsun)

빈 잔에는 고독만 bin ja-ne-neun go-dong-man
있는 것이 아니다 it-neun geo-si a-ni-da

설움도 있고 seo-lum-do it-go
그리움도 같이 있다 geu-rium-do ga-chi it-da

새벽녘 sae-byeong nyeok
달빛, 별빛도 dal-bit, byeol-bit-do
바닥에 묻어 있다 ba-da-ge mu-deo it-da

Mother 34

Sin Wungsun

It is not to existent

Only solitude in an empty glass.

There are also together

Grieve and yearning in that one.

At that dawn,

The moon light, the star light,

Are covered on the floor, too.

시조時調 (sijo)

이 석 규(Lee Seokgyu)

바람 속 내 영혼이
ba-ram ssok nae yeong-ho-ni
이삭처럼 여무는 곳
i-sak-cheo-reom yeo-mu-neun got
사思와 감感을 모아 담는
sa-wa ga-meul mo-a dam-neun
가장 작은 오지그릇
ga-jang ja-geun o-ji geu-reut
겨레의
gyeo-re-ui
만년 숨결이
man-nyeon sum-gyeol-ri
혈관 속을 돌고 있다
hyeol-gwan so-geul dol-go it-da

Sijo

Lee Seokgyu

Where my spirit in the wind
Ripens like the ears of rice,
The smallest pottery that
Put in thinking and feeling,
Brotherly
Perpetual breathing
has been running in the vein.

와송臥松 (wa-song)

김 낙 기(Kim Nakgi)

늙은 솔 거친 등걸
neul-geun sol geo-chin deung-geol
외로 누운 산턱 어디
oe-ro nu-un san-teok eo-di
운무와 벗한 세월
un-mu-wa beot-han se-wol
가지 더러 고사된 채
ga-ji deo-reo go-sa-doen chae
이끼는 겉주름 피고 i-kki-neun
외솔 잎만 oe-sol im-man
예제 yeo-je
한 둘 han dul.

A pine lied on

Kim Nakgi

The rough trunk of an old pine,
Where of a hill lied on its side,
Times made friends with cloud and fog,
Some boughs remain died,
The lichen is in bloom the wrinkle,
Only pine leaves
Here, there
One, two.

노을 (no-eul)

오 세 영(O Seyeong)

은하에 홍수 일어
eun-ha-e hong-su I-reo
강물이 범람했나.
gang-mu-ri beom-ram haen-na
하늘 한 모서리가
ha-neul han mo-seo-ri-ga
황톳물에 젖어있다.
hwang-to-mul-re jeo-jeo it-da
견우의 모내기 논도
gyeon-u-ui mo-nae-gi non-do
큰 수해를 입었겠다.
keun su-hae-reul i-beot-geot-da.

A sunset glow

O Seyeong

The flood got up in the Galaxy,
Did the river water overflow,
A coner of the sky is getting wet
With water of yellow soil
The rice-planting field of the Altair, too
Would suffer big damage by a flood.

청靑 (cheong)

한 분 순(Han Bunsun)

여름은 yeo-reu-meun
내 곁에 nae-gyeo-tae
아직 무성(茂盛)히 있네 a-jik mu-seong-i in-ne

깊숙한 골짜기에서 gip-suk-han gol-jja-gi-e-seo
한잠 자고 han-jam ja-go
이내를 건너 i-nae-reul geon-neo

더러는 deo-reo-neun
빠뜨리고 더러는 ppa-tteu-ri-go deo-reo-neun
또 손에도 들었네. tto son-e-do deu-reon-ne.

Blue

Han Bunsun

Summer, at my side,
Yet, is luxuriantly,

In the secluded valley,
It gets a sleep,
Goes across this stream,

Somewhat
Drops in, somewhat
Hold also in my hands.

노송老松 (no-song)

정 순 량(Jeong, Soonryang)

등 굽은 시골 할미
deung gu-beun si-gol hal-mi
살아온 여정처럼
sa-ra-on- yeo-jeong-cheo-reom
산 비알 바위틈에
san-bial ba-wi-teum-e
바람 맞서 버틴 세월
ba-ram mat-seo beo-tin se-wol
자세는 구부정해도
ja-se-neun gu-bu-jeong-hae-do
짙푸른 저 당당함.
jit-pu-reun jeo dang-dang ham

An old pine tree

Jeong Soonryang

As journey a rural granny
Bent her back has been lived,
At the gap of a mount's rock,
It is time endured against wind.
Amazing, though its' posture curve,
There is a dark blue dignity.

백담 설악 (bakdam seo-rak)

홍 성 란(Hong, Seongran)

너처럼 초대받은 neo-cheo-reom cho-dae ba-deun
손님 1, 2, 3이다만 son-nim il, i, sa-mi da-man

이 산, 이 계곡이 i-san, i gye-go-gi
내 것인 양 흐뭇해 nae geo-sin-yang heu-mu-tae

어떠랴 eo-tteo-rya
주인으로 행세하면, ju-in-eu-ro haeng-se-ha-myeon,
스쳐가는 행인이 seu-cheo-ga-neun haeng-i-ni.

BaekDam Seor-ak

Hong, Seongran

Though I am one of the guests
One, two, three invited like you,

This Mountain, this valley gratify me as mine,

How about
As acting as a hostess,
Though passerby goes by.

절정 (jeol-jeong)

김 복 근(Kim, Bokgeun)

산천재 남명매
san-cheon-jae nam-myeong mae
꽃망울 벙그는 소리
kkon-mang-ul beong-geu-neun so-ri

소주 첫잔을
so-ju cheot-ja-neul
비울 때 동동이는 소리
bi-ul-ttae dong-dong-i-neun so-ri

가을 볕
gae-eul byeot
뜨거운 햇살
tteu-geo-un haet-sal
콩꼬투리
kong kko-tu-ri
터지는 소리
teo-ji-neun so-ri

The acme

Kim, Bokgeun

It's the sound
That flower buds are blooming
In Sancheonjae, Nammyeongmae,

It's the sound
Drinking to the dreg the first hard liquor glass

It's the sound
That the autumn sunshine,
Hot sunlight,
Bean pods are bursting out.

어머니 (eo-meo-ni)

차 도 연(Cha, Doyeon)

입 안에 맴돌리다 i-bane maem-dol-ri-da
삼켜버린 sam-kyeo beo-rin
아! 그 이름 a! geu I-reum

가슴 속 깊은데서 ga-seum sok gi-peun-de-seo
큰 불씨로 되살아나 keun bul-ssi-ro doe-sa-ra-na

뻘겋게 ppeol-geo-ke
피어오르며 pi-eo-o-reu-myeo
눈시울을 덥힌다. nun-si-u-reul deo-pin-da.

Mother

Cha, Doyeon

Spinning round it in my mouth,
Swallowed,
Aha! the name,

Resuscitating with a big kindling in my deep heart,

With bright red,
Beginning to grow
The eye rims are moved to tears.

가을 (gae-eul)

김 인 자(Kim, Inja)

한 폭의 그림 속엔 han po-gui geu-rim so-gen
정갈한 바람소리 jeong-gal-han ba-ram so-ri

황홀한 가을 햇살 hwang-hol-han ga-eul hat-sal
한 잎의 낙엽 되어 han ni-pui na-gyeob doe-eo

저무는 jeo-mu-neun
세월 끝에서 se-wol kkeu-te-seo
세상 이치 깨닫네. se-sang I-chi kkae-dan-ne.

Autumn

Kim, Inja

The inside of a picture
Neat and clean sound of the wind.

Ecstatic sun light of fall
Become a fallen leaf,

To get dark,
At the edge of the times,
I see the reason of the world.

도리깨를 보며 (do-ri-kkae-reul bo-myeo)

이 광 녕(Lee, Gwangnyeong)

돌려 패고 찍어 팬다 dol-ryeo pae-go jji-geo paen-da
세상 시름 갈기갈기 se-sang si-reum gal-gi gal-gi

한풀이의 마당 같은 han-pu-ri-ui madang ga-teun
땀방울의 전설 같은 ttam-bang-u-rui jeon-seol ga-teun

고향집 go-hyang-jip
등 굽은 향수가 deung gu-beun hyang-su-ga
검불 쓰고 손짓한다. geom-bul sseu-go son-jit-handa

To see a flail

Lee, Gwangnyeong

Turning and beating, cut and thresh
World anxiety comes to pieces

As a garden of its grudge
As a legend of a sweat drop,

On my home,
Missing nostalgia
Shakes hands for me with pine straw.

그리운 잔盞 (geu-ri-un jan)

유 재 영(Yu, Jaeyeong)

한 방울 한 방울씩

han bang-ul-ssik

가슴 깊이 스며들어

ga-seum gi-pi seu-myeo deu-reo

누굴까 내게 와서

nu-gul-kka nae-ge wa-seo

잔이 된 그 사람은

jan-i-doen gui sa-ra-meun

공손히 두 손 모으고

gong-son-hi du son mo-eu-go

받아드는 떨림이여.

ba-da-deu-neun tteol-rim-i-yeo

A missing glass

Yu, Jaeyeong

A drop by a drop,
He permeated deeply in my heart.
Who is him, he came me, and
He became a pretty glass.
Politely, the quaver taking
With my two hands together.

제3부

해오리 꿈을 찾다
hae-ori-reul chat-da

한재희 Han, Jaehui

삼무의 온천수에
sam-mu-ui on-cheon-su-e
오욕을 씻어내니
o-yo-geul ssi-seo nae-ni

까마귀 백로 되어
kka-ma-gwi baeng-no doe-eo
조령고개 넘나들며
jo-ryeong go-gae neom-na-deul-myeo

청운의
cheong-un-ui
과거길 찾아
goa-geo gil cha-ja
선비정신 새긴다.
seon-bi jeong-sin sae-gin-da

다문화 가족 (da-mun-hwa ga-jok)

류 각 현(Ryu, Gakhyeon)

화원을 더 예쁘게
hwa-wo-neul deo ye-bbeu-ge
물주고 가꾸면서
mul ju-go ga-kku-myeon-seo

우리는 서로 다른
uri-neun seo-ro da-reun
아름다운 꽃이 되어
a-reum-da-un kko-chi doe-eo

활짝 핀 웃음꽃 함께
hwal-jjak-pin u-seom-kkot ham-kke
어깨춤을 두둥실.
eo-kkae-chu-meul du-dung-sil

The multi-cultural family

Ryu, Gakhyeon

Raising and watering
prettier the flower garden,

We become beautiful flowers
Each other different,

Together smile flowers in full bloom,
We dance Dudungsil by shoulder.

* Dudungsil: Korean language, onomatopoeia.

해오리 꿈을 찾다 (hae-ori-reul chat-da)

한 재 희(Han, Jaehui)

삼무의 온천수에
sam-mu-ui on-cheon-su-e
오욕을 씻어내니
o-yo-geul ssi-seo nae-ni

까마귀 백로 되어
kka-ma-gwi baeng-no doe-eo
조령고개 넘나들며
jo-ryeong go-gae neom-na-deul-myeo

청운의
cheong-un-ui
과거길 찾아
goa-geo gil cha-ja
선비정신 새긴다.
seon-bi jeong-sin sae-gin-da

A white heron finds a dream

Han, Jaehui

Washing five avarice
With the water of King's Spa

A crow turns out a white heron,
Going and coming Joryeong ridge,

Looking for
The high rank's exam road
And engraves a scholar mind

왕의 온천 (wang-ui on-cheon)

박 근 모(Bak Keunmo)

암반 속 am-ban sok
심층에서 sim-cheung-e-seo
뿜어낸 광천수로 ppu-meo-naen gwang-cheon-su-ro

과거 길 지친 발을 gwa-geo gil ji-chin ba-reul
풀어주던 신비한 물 pu-reo-ju-deon sin-bi-han mul

희망과 hi-mang-gwa
건강의 성지 geon-gang-ui seong-ji
왕의 온천 수안보.wang-ui on-cheon suanbo

King's Spa

Bak Keunmo

In base rock,
In the depths
Mineral water gushed out,

Mysterious water released
The tired feet of Gwa Geo road,

The desire,
The health's holy land,
It's the king's hot spring, Su An Bo.

한 때, 꽃 (han ttae, kkot)

민 병 도(Min, Byeongdo)

네가 시드는 건 ne-ga si-deu-neun-geon
네 잘못이 아니다 ne jal-mo-si a-ni-da

아파하지 말아라 a-pa-ha-ji ma-ra-ra
시드니까 꽃이다 si-deu-ni-kka kko-chi-da

누군들 nu-gun-deul
살아 한 때 꽃, sa-la han ttae kkot
아닌 적이 있었던가 a-nin jeo-gi i-sseo-deon-ga

At one time, flower

Min, Byeongdo

It is not your fault
That you have now withered.

Do not feel a pain it.
Now that it withers is flower.

Anyone,
At one time in one's life,
All was beautiful flower.

7월 어느 날 (7wol eo-neu nal)

고 현 숙(Go, Hyeonsuk)

뜨락에 좌선하듯 tteu-ra-ge jwa-seon-ha-deut
조용히 앉은 햇살 jo-yong-hi an-jeun haet-sal

새들도 날아들다 sae-deul-do na-ra-deul-da
숲으로 숨어드는 su-peuro su-meo-deu-neun

태우다 재만 남을 듯 tae-u-da jae-man nam-eul deut
불이 붙은 여름 날. bu-li bu-teun yeo-reum-nal

July, one day

Go, Hyeonsuk

Meditating in the garden,
The sunlight sitting quietly,

Birds also come flying
And hiding into forest,

Remaining only ashes burned,
It makes fire summer day.

휴화산 (hyu-hwa-san)

양 계 향(Yang Gyehyang)

천지를 뒤흔드는 cheon-ji-reul dwi-heun-deu-neun
불길을 뿜었었지 bul-gi-reul ppu-meo-seot-ji

들끓는 용암으로 deul-kkeul-neun yong-a-meu-ro
큰 굴도 뚫었었지 keun gul-do ddu-reo-seot-ji

다시 올 그날을 위해 da-si ol geu-na-reul ui-hae
숨죽이고 있구나. sum-ju-gi-go it-gu-na

A dormant volcano

Yang Gyehyang

Shaking a world violently,
It had erupted into flame.

With the boiling lava jet,
It had digged through big cave.

For a vital day to come again,
It is with breathless quietly.

길 (gil)

권 갑 하(Gwon, Gabha)

닿지도 da-chi-do
멎지도 못한 meot-ji-do mo-tan
오랜 배회의 날들 o-raen bae-hoe-ui nal-deul

스스로 seu-seu-ro
몸을 누이며 mo-meul nu-i-myeo
지워오는 점점의 소실 ji-wo-o-neun jeom-jeom-ui so-sil

칠흑 속 chil-heuk-sok
눈뜬 길 하나 nun-tteun gil ha-na
갈수록 향기롭다. gal-su-rok hyang-gi-rob-da

A way

Gwon, Gabha

Not reaching
Or not stopping,
It's days of my long wandering,

On my own
Lying on my back
And erasing vanity.

A way opened in a coal-black,
As times go on, it is fragrant.

망향 (mang-hyang)

문 복 선(Mun, Bokseon)

남풍이 고운 날엔 nam-pung-i go-un na-ren
언덕에 올라본다 eon-deo-ge ol-ra bon-da
오월은 청보리 물결 o-wo-reun cheong-bo-ri mul-gyeol
물오르는 부푼 가슴 mul-o-reu-neun bu-pun ga-seum
하이얀 감꽃 향기를 ha-i-yan gam-kkot hyang-gi-reul
목에 걸던 소녀야 mo-ge geol-deon so-nyeo-ya

110 * 빗방울 A raindrop

Nostalgia

Mun, Bokseon

I climb up a hillock
When a gentle breeze is blowing.
May is the wave of blue barley,
It is buoyant heart with the sap.
The perfume of white persimmon,
A girl worn around her neck.

그러려니 (geu-ryeo-yeo-ni)

김 석 철(Gim, Seokcheol)

본 것도 못 본 듯이 bon geo-tto mot bon-deu-si
없는 것도 있는 듯이 eom-neun geo-tto it-neun-deu-si
할 말도 줄이면서 hal mal-do ju-ri myeon-seo
욕심일랑 삭히면서 yoksim ilrang sa-kimyeonseo
하 세월 그 깊은 철학 ha se-wol geu gi-peun cheol-hak
포용하고 사느니. po-yong-ha-go sa-neu-ni.

Yes, it is so

Gim, Seokcheol

As not to see things I see,
As I have things I do not have,
Reducing a talk to do,
Digesting self-interest,
Long long times,
I live tolerating the deep philosophy.

봄비 (bom-bi)

나 순 옥(Na, Sun-ok)

은침 하나하나 eun-chim ha-na ha-na
맥을 짚어 꽂는다 mae-geul ji-peo kkon-neun da

찬란한 태몽 앞에 chal-ran-han tae-mong a-pe
밀려나가는 냉중 mil-ryeo-na-ga-neun naeng-jeung

대지는 dae-ji-neun
몸을 뒤틀며 mo-meul dwi-teul-myeo
입덧이 한창이다 ip-deo-si han-chang-i-da

Spring rain

Na, Sun-ok

Silver needles, one by one
Are pinned feeling earth's pulse.

In front of brilliant Taemong胎夢*,
Coldness is been pushing out.

Mother earth,
Withing Her body,
Suffers from morning sickness.

* Taemong胎夢 : Korean language, the meaning is a dream of
   forthcoming conception.

분수 (bun-su)

김 사 균(Gim, Sagyun)

여름 날 땡볕하늘 yeo-reum nal ttaeng-byeot ha-neul
안개꽃이 피는 공원 an-gae-kko-chi pi-neun gong-won

이무기 용이 되어 i-mu-gi yong-i doe-eo
구름 잡아 승천한다 gu-reum ja-ba seung-cheon han-da

안개꽃 사이사이로 an-gae-kkot sai-sai-ro
키가 크는 무지개. ki-ga keu-neun mu-ji-gae.

A fountain

Gim, Sagyun

A summer day, a hot sky,
In the park the haze-flowers bloom

A boa became a dragon,
Ascends to heaven to take the cloud.

A tall rainbow looking better
Remarkably among the flowers.

소금 (so-geum)

조 주 환(Jo, Juwhan)

푸르게 살아 끓던
pu-reu-ge sa-ra kkeul-teon
피와 살은 다 빠지고
pi-wa sal-eun da ppa-ji-go
조각난 유리 같은
jo-gang-nan yuri gateun
저 투명한 물의 뼈가
jeo tu-myeong-han mu-rui ppyeo-ga
마지막
ma-ji-mak
지상에 남아
ji-sang-e na-ma
혼의 불로 타고 있다.
hon-ui bul-ro ta-go it-da.

Salt

Jo, Juwhan

Blood and flesh that lived on vividly,

Drain off all together,

The bone of transparent water

Like a glass splinter,

The final,

Remaining on the ground,

It is burning by fire of soul.

징검돌 (jing geom dol)

김 일 영(Kim Ilyeong)

머물다 흐르다가 meo-mul-da heu-reu-daga
굽이친 여울물에 gu-bi-chin yeo-ul mu-re

하나 둘 디딤돌로 ha-na dul di-dim dol-ro
희망을 품다보면 hui-mang-eul pum-da bo-myeon
어느새 eo-neu-sae
스쳐간 바람 seu-chyeo-gan ba-ram
서리꽃을 피우고. seo-kko-cheul pi-u-go.

Stepping stones

Kim Ilyeong

Remaining and flowing by
A turning water of rapids

Put stepping stones one by one
Entertaining ambition

Unaware,
Wind pass by swiftly
Makes a pretty frost-flower open.

석국 (seok-guk)

성 철 용(Seong, Cheolyong)

예 놀던 선비 모셔
ye nol-deon seon-bi mo-syeo
우리 둘 다 신선되어
u-ri dul-da sin-seon doe-eo
선비는 옛날 걸고
seon-bi-neun yen-nal geol-go
자신은 오늘 걸고
ja-sin-eun o-neul geol-go
사인암 sa-in-am
보는 앞에서 bo-neun a-pe-seo
바둑 한 판 두고 싶다.
ba-duk han pan du-go sip-da.

The game of baduk

Seong, Cheolyong

Attending a scholar played in old times
We both become wizards,
The scholar stakes ancient,
I make a deposit of today,
In the front of that Sain rock is seeing
I want to play a game of baduk.

점자를 읽다 (jeom-ja-reul ik-da)

김 영 주(Kim, Yeong-ju)

너에게로 가는 길이 neo-e-ge-ro gan-eun gi-ri
내 마음에 놓인 길이 nae ma-eum-e no-in gi-ri

손닿고 싶었다고 son-da-ko si-peot-da-go
귀엣말 하고 싶다고 hwi-en-mal ha-go sip-da-go

가까이 ga-kka-i
더 가까이 오라며 deo ga-kka-i o-ra-myeo
두드리는 더듬이 du-du-ri-neun deo-deu-mi

Braille type is read

Kim, Yeong-ju

The way going to you;
The way laid in my mind,

I would like to touch hand;
I would like to whisper your ears,

Near at hand,
Coming nearer at hand,
It is striking its fumble.

제4부

말의 무게 mal-ui mu-ge

주강식 Ju gang sik

거짓말의 무게는 1g,
geo-jin mal-ui mu-ge-neun il-gram
선생의 말은 5g,
seon-saeng-ui mal-eun o-gram

노인 말은 0g,
no-in-ui mal-eun yong gram
자식 말은 1톤,
ja-sik mal-eun il-ton

모든 말 부도난 시대에
mo-deun mal bu-do-nan si-dae-e
자식 말만 무겁다.
ja-sik ma-lman mu-geob-da.

개나리 (gaenari)

하 경 민(Ha, Kyeongmin)

샛노랑 봄소식에 saen nor-ang bom-so-si-ge
희망이 주렁주렁 hui-mang-i ju-reong ju-reong

새봄의 전령사가 sae-bom-ui jeol-ryeong-sa-ga
우리들 가슴속에 u-ri-deul ga-seum so-ge

그리운 봄의 향기를 geu-ri-un bom-ui hyang-gi-reul
가슴 가득 안겨준다. ga-seum ga-deuk an-gyeo jun-da

A forsythia

Ha, Kyeongmin

In the deep yellow news of spring,
It has borne abundant hope,

To be messenger of spring,
It is existent in our heart.

You are being embraced in full arms
Longing fragrance of spring.

모 초 (mocho)

이 일 향(Lee Ilhyang)

세우면 한 폭 깃발 se-um-yeon han pok gi-ppal
눕히면 푸른 강물 nu-pi-myeon pu reun gang-mul
생각은 가뭇없이 saeng-ga-geun ga-mut eop-si
하늘 밖에 저무는데 ha-neul ba-kke jeo-mu-neun-de
慕情(모정)은 mo-jeong eun
열 두 폭 치마 yeol du pok chi-ma
심고 섰는 파초여라. sim-go seon-neun pa-cho-yeo-ra.

A plantain

Lee Ilhyang

Being set up, It is a banner.
Laying down, It is blue river.
Thinking is out of sight,
Remaining out of sky
Affection
Is a twelve-leaf skirt,
A planting, standing plantain.

가족탕 (ga-jok-tang)

심 웅 문(Sim, eungmun)

한 가족 벌거숭이 han ga-jok beol-geo-sung-i
네 식구가 탕에 있다. ne sik-gu-ga tang-e it-da

남매는 어리지만 nam-mae-neun eo-ri-ji-man
내 후년엔 못 오겠네 nae hu-nyeon-en mot o-gen-ne

서로의 등을 밀면서 seo-ro-ui deung-eul mil-myeon seo
하하 호호 껄껄껄. ha ha ho ho kkeol kkeol kkeol.

A family bath

Sim, eungmun

One family of naked,
Four persons are in the bath.

Though brother, sister are infant,
They will not come later years.

Scrubbing softly each other's backs
Haha, Hoho, kkeol, kkeol, kkeol.

유채꽃 보며-心法·36
(yu-chae kko-cheul bo-myeo)

오 종 문(Oh Jongmun)

그 마을 돌개바람 geu ma-eul dol-gae-ba-ram
써레질로 끄는 봄날 sseo-re-jil-ro kkeu-neun bom-nal)

노란 물감 풀어 놓은 no-ran mul-gam pu-reo no-eun
누군가의 따듯한 손 nu-gun-ga-ui tta-deu-tan son

진실을 하늘로 믿고 jin-si-reul ha-neu-lro mit-go

그 땅처럼 사는 것 geu ttang-cheo-reom sa-neun geot

Watching rape flowers

Oh Jongmun

Whirlwinds of the village,
Spring day pulling in by sweeping,

A warm hand of someone released a yellow paint

It is to believe the truth by heaven,
It is to live as the ground.

봄 (bom)

고 동 우(Go, Dongwoo)

물 오른 팔 한껏 뻗어
mul o-reun pal han-kkeot ppeo-deo
하늘을 끌어안은
ha-neu-reul kkeu-reo-a-neun

곧추 선 겨울 나목
go-chu seon gyeo-ul na-mok
묵은 숨 토해낸다
mu-geun sum to-hae naen-da

온 산이 요가 하는 구나
on san-i yoga ha-neun gu-na
연두 빛 핏기 돌겠다.
yeon-du-bit pit-gi dol-get-da.

Spring

Go, Dongwoo

The sap of trees make their arms
At full stretch to hug the sky.

Erect winter bare woods
Regurgitate old breathes.

All mountain is doing Yoga.
Yellow green of blood is circulating.

마루거울 (ma-ru geo-ul)

최 길 하(Cheoi Gilha)

어머닌 칠흑 같은 eo-meo-nin chil-heuk-ga-teun
마루를 닦으시며 ma-ru-reul da-kkeu-simyeo
세상의 모든 것이 se-sang-ui mo-deun geo-si
거울이라 하시었다 geo-ul-i-ra ha-si-eot-da
如來는 yeo-rae-neun
한 육신이 다 han yuk-si-ni da
빛이 되게 닦으셨다. bi-chi- doe-ge da-kkeu-syeot-da.

The floor mirror

Cheoi Gilha

Mother had been polishing,
The floor like jet, and said that
Everything of the world is a mirror.

Buddhist saint
Had been cultivated
So that a body all became light.

금정산에 올라 (geum jeong san-e ol-ra)

임 종 찬(Yim, Jongchan)

이 세상 옷을 입고
i-se-sang o-seul ip-go
오십 넘게 살았건만
o-sip neom-ge sa-rat-geon-man
꽃피고 잎 지듯이
kkot-pi-go ip ji-deu-si
세상사는 법을 몰라
se-sang sa-neun beo-beul mol-la
가끔씩 금정산에 올라
ga-kkeum-ssik geum-jeong-san-e ol-la
나를 던져 놓는다.
na-reul deon-jyeo non-neun-da.

To climb at the Geumjeongsan

Yim, Jongchan

Wearing the clothes of this world,
Though I live in over fifty years,
As flowers bloom and leaves droop,
Not to know law to live the world,
Sometimes to climb at the Geumjeongsan,
I put to throw myself there.

오늘도 태양은 둥근데
(o-neul-do tae-yang-eun dung-geun-de)

서 길 석(Seo, Gilseok)

인생은 나그네라
in-saeng-eun na-geu-ne-ra
철학적 화두 앞에
cheol-hak-jeok hwa-du a-pe

모두가 나그네면
mo-du-ga na-geu-ne-myeon
주인은 누구인가
ju-i-neun nu-gu-in-ga

태양은 늘 둥근 것을
tae-yang-eun neul dung-geun geo-seul
길다 짧다 탓하네.
gil-da jjal-da ta-ta-ne

The sun is round

Seo, Gilseok

Life is the wayfarer,
In front of the philosophical topic,

If all of us is the farer,
Who is the owner

'The Sun is always round' however,
People complain it is long or short.

정이 들면 (jeong-i-deul-myeon)

함 세 린(Ham, Serin)

눈앞에 보여지는 nun-a-pe bo-yeo ji-neun
세상의 모든 것들 se-sang-ui mo-deun geot-deul

눈감고 보여지는 nun-gam-go bo-yeo-ji-neun
마음속 이야기들 ma-eum-sok I-ya-gi-deul

보고도 알지 못하나 bo-go-do al-ji-mo-ta-na
안보고도 아는 일. an bo-go-do a-neun-il

Fall in love

Ham, Serin

All the things of the world
Showing on the front of eyes,

Stories which is in my mind
Seen with your eyes closed,

Though I have seen, but I don't know,
Without seeing, knowing thing.

말의 무게 (mal-ui mu-ge)

주 강 식(Ju gang sik)

거짓말의 무게는 1g,

geo-jin mal-ui mu-ge-neun il-gram

선생의 말은 5g,

seon-saeng-ui mal-eun o-gram

노인 말은 0g,

no-in-ui mal-eun yong gram

자식 말은 1톤,

ja-sik mal-eun il-ton

모든 말 부도난 시대에

mo-deun mal bu-do-nan si-dae-e

자식 말만 무겁다.

ja-sik ma-lman mu-geob-da.

The weight of the word

Ju, Kangsik

The weight of a falsehood is one gram
The teacher's remarks are five gram

The aged's talk is zero gram
The child's word is one ton.

In the times that all the words are dishonored
The child's saying only is heavy.

마음의 무게 (ma-eum-ui mu-ge)

김 숙 선(Kim, Sookseon)

잔잔한 호수 가에 jan-jan-han ho-su ga-e
누군가 돌을 던져 nu-gun-ga do-reul deon-jyeo
일렁인 파장 위에 il-reong-in pa-jang wi-e
가슴앓이 떨림으로 ga-seum-a-ri tteol-rim-eu-ro
시이소 si-i-so
타는 너와나 ta-neun neo-wa na
오고가는 추(錐)인가. o-go-ga-neun chu-in-ga.

Heft of mind

Kim, Sookseon

Someone threw

A stone into the calm lake without thinking,

With heartburn trembling

On the wavelength waved,

You and I,

Riding on the "up and down ,

Are the weight Coming and going?

거울 (geo-ul)

홍 오 선(Hong, Ohsun)

만 년 전 전생의 나
man nyeon jeon jeon-saeng-ui na
만년 후 후생의 나
man-nyeon hu hu-saeng-ui na
그 사이 내가 앉아
geu sa-i nae-ga an-ja
지금의 날 바라보네.
ji-geum-ui nal ba-ra-bo-ne
턱없이
teog-eop-si
작아진 모습
ja-ga-jin mo-seup
부끄러워 돌아앉네.
bu-kkeu-reo-wo do-ra an-ne.

Mirror

Hong, Ohsun

My figure of long ago,
My looks of long after,
I look over me on the present
Sitting down between them,
Extremely,
With my lessened looks,
I am ashamed of myself.

촌부일기 (chon-bu il-gi)

김 보 영(Kim, Boyeong)

가슴에 일던 바람

ga-seum-e il-deon ba-ram

텃밭에 묻어 두고

teot-ba-te mu-deo du-go

밭두렁 들꽃처럼

ba-ttu-reong deul-kkot-cheo-reom

허드레 핀 풀꽃 되어

heo-deu-re pin pul-kkot-doe-eo

늦가을

neut-ga-eul

봉당에 앉아

bong-dang-e an-ja

빛 한 줄기 안고 싶네.

bit-tan-jeul-gi an-go-sim-ne.

A country woman diary

Kim, Boyeong

Burying at the kitchen garden
The wind risen in my heart,
As wild flowers at the ridge of field,
becoming grass flowers odds blown,
The late fall,
Sitting on the floor,
I want to hug a streak of light.

벽에 걸린 웃음 (byeok-e geol-rin u-seum)

정 진 상(Jeong jin sang)

입 꼬리 귀에 붙은 ip kko-ri gwi-e bu-teun

벽에 걸린 사진 한 장 byeok-e geol-rin sa-jin han jang

꽁꽁 언 나의 가슴 kkong kkong eon na-ui gas-eum

어루만져 사르르 eo-ru man-jyeo sa-reu-reu

봄바람 bom-ba-ram

불어오시네 bu-reo o-sine

겨울에도 불어오네. gyeo-u-redo bu-reo o-sine.

A smile hung on the wall

Jeong, Ginsang

A picture*hung on the wall
With a smile spreading over her face,
It melt to stroke softly with smile
My heart frozen thickly.
The spring wind
blows from the photograph,
Blows also in the winter.

* granddaughter's picture.

촛불 (chot-bul)

김 광 수 (Kim, Gwangsu)

스치는 바람에도 seu-chi-neun ba-ra-me-do
아린 넋을 추슬러 a-rin neok-seul chu-seul-reo
한사코 어둠 내몰며 han-sa-ko eo-dum nae-mol-myeo
애태우던 우리 어머니 ae-tae-u-deon u-ri eo-meo-ni
사위고 남은 심지엔 sa-wi-go nam-eun sim-ji-en
눈물만이 엉기었네. nun-mul-ma-ni eong-gi-eon-ne.

A candlelight

Kim, Gwangsu

Even a line grazing wind,
To handle tingling spirit,
To the death, to expel darkness,
My mother had bothered.
Burn it out,
At the remaining wick,
The only tears coagulated.

제5부

진달래 연가
jin-dal-rae yeon-ga

이태극 Lee Taegeuk

철길 가 흐드러진
cheol-gil-ga heu-deu-reo-jin
함박웃음 밀물로 와
ham-bak u-seum mil-mul-ro wa
연분홍 맺힌 사연
yeon-bun-hong mae-chin sa-yeon
찾아 드는 이 오후는
cha-ja -deu-neu i-o-hu-neun
스치는 꽃샘바람도
seu-chi-neun kkot-saem-ba-ram-do
가슴 깊이 안긴다.
ga-seum gi-pi an-gin-da.

자모사 (ja-mo-sa)

정 인 보(Jeong Inbo)

가을은 그 가을이
ga-eu-reun geu ga-eu-ri
바람 불고 잎 드는데
ba-ram bul-go ip deu-neun-de
가신 님·어이하여
ga-sin-nim eo-i-ha-yeo
돌·오실 줄 모르는가
dol o-sil-jul mo-reu-neun-ga
살뜰히 기르신 아이
sal-tteul-ri gi-reu-sin a-i
옷 품 준 줄 아소서.
ot pum jun jul a-so-seo.

Mother in retrospect

Jeong Inbo

A autumn, the autumn,
The wind blows and leaves fall.
Why didn't the late mother
Know to come back,
Know your child brought up frugally,
His clothes to be small size.

봄 (bom)

이 은 상(Lee Eunsang)

매화꽃 졌다 하신 편지를 받자옵고
mae-hwa-kkot jeot-da hasin
pyeon-ji-reul bat-ja-op-go
개나리 한창이란 답장을 보내었소
gae-na-ri han-chang-i-ran
dap-jang-eul bo-nae-eot so
이 둘 다 봄이란 말을 차마 쓰기 어려워서.
I- dul-da bo-miran mal-eul
cha-ma sseu-gi eo-ryeo-wo-seo

Spring

Lee Eunsang

Receiving your letter written,
'The ume flowers had fallen'
Sending my reply letter,
'At the height of the forsythia'
All these two;
It was difficult truly to write 'spring' the word.

석류 (seong-yu)

조 운(Jo Un)

투박한 나의 얼굴 두툼한 나의 입술

tu-ba-kan na-ui eol-gul

du-tum-han na-ui ip-sul

알알이 붉은 뜻을 내가 어이 이르리까

al-al-ri bul-geun tteu-seul

nae-ga eo-i i-reu-ri-kka

보소라 임아 보소라 빠개 젖힌 이 가슴.

bo-so-ra i-ma bo-so-ra

ppa-gae jyeo-chin i-ga-seum.

A pomegranate

Jo Un

The rustic of my feature,
And pretty of my full lips,
Gram by gram, the scarlet mind
How can I say to my sweetheart,
Look at me, my loving honey,
Look in my heart be opened.

석류 (seong-yu)

이 희 승(Lee Huiseung)

잎 속에 반만 숨어 푸른 하늘 쳐다보고
ip so-ge ban-man su-meo
pu-reun ha-neul cheo-da bo-go
그 뺨이 그 입술이 새빨갛게 타오르네
geu ppya-mi geu ip-su-ri
sae-ppal-ga-ke ta-o-reu-ne
이보오 겉만 그런가 속도 헤쳐 보임세.
i-bo-o geon-man geu-reon-ga
sok-do he-cheo bo-im-se.

The pomegranate

Lee Huiseung

Hiding only half in the leaves
Looking up at the blue sky.
Its cheek, its lip
Blaze up deep red.
Hey, is the appearance only like that,
See turning up its inside too.

난 (nan)

이 호 우(Lee Howoo)

벌 · 나빈 알리 없는 깊은 산 곳을 가려
beol na-bin al-ri eom-neun
gi-peun san go-seul ga-ryeo
안으로 다스리는 청자빛 맑은 향기
an-eu-ro da-seu-ri-neun
cheong-ja-bit mal-geun hyang-gi
종이에 물이 스미듯 미소 같은 정이여.
jong-i-e muri seu-mi-deut
miso ga-teun jeong-i-yeo.

Orchid

Lee Howoo

Bees, butterflies could not know,
what live in the deep mountain.
Celadon green, clear fragrance managing inside,
As water sink into paper,
It is smile of affection.

난초 (nan-cho)

이 병 기(Lee Byeonggi)

빼어난 가는 잎 새 굳은 듯 보드랍고
ppae-eo-nan ga-neun ip-sae
gu-deun deut bo-deu-rap-go)
자줏빛 굵은 대공 하이얀 꽃이 벌고
ja-ju-bit gul-geun dae-gong
ha-i-yan kko-chi beol-go
이슬은 구슬이 되어 마디마디 달렸다.
i-seu-reun gu--seu-ri doe-eo
ma-di ma-di dal-ryeot-da.

An orchid

Lee Byeonggi

The excellent, slender leaves
Are tender as adamant,
On the thick stalk of purple
Becomes open white flowers.
The dew became a band of glass beads,
Hung on every joint of the stem.

단 란 (dal-ran)

이 영 도(Lee Youngdo)

아이는 글을 읽고, a-i-neun geul-reul il-kko,
나는야 수를 놓고 na-neun-ya su-reul no-ko

심지를 돋우고서, sim-ji-reul do-du-go-seo,
이마를 맞대이면 i-ma-reul mat-dae-i-myeon

어둠도 eo-dum-do
고운 애정에 go-un ae-jeong-e
삼가는 듯 둘렸다 sam-ga-neun deut dul-ryeot-da.

Happy

Lee Youngdo

The child is reading writings,
I am making embroidery,

Being turned up the wick,
laying foreheads together,

The dark too,
Be encircled carefully
By the beautiful affection.

봉선화 (bong-seon-hwa)

김 상 옥(Kim Sang-ok)

비 오자 장독간에 봉선화 반만 벌어
bi-o-ja jang-dok-gan-e
bong-seon-hwa ban-man beo-reo
해마다 피는 꽃을 나만 두고 볼 것인가
hae-ma-da pi-neun kko-cheul
na-man du-go bol-geo-sin-ga
세세한 사연을 적어 누님께로 보내자
se-se-han sa-yeon-reul jeo-geo
nu-nim-kke-ro bo-nae-ja.

The balsam

Kim Sang-ok

Just after It rains, at the terrace*
The balsams half opened.
Year by year, flowers coming out
Do I only see them.
Let's it send
My elder sister
Writing contents minutely,

*the soy jar terrace,(Korean :Jangdogdae)

어머니 (eo-meo-ni)

박 병 순(Bak Byeongsun)

눈 펑펑 쏟아지는 사 십리 새벽길을

nun peong-peong sso-da-ji-neun

sa sim-ri sae-byeok-gi-reul

그렇게 뿌리쳐도 싸 주시던 그 보따리

geu-reo-ke ppuri-chyeo-do

ssa ju-si-deon geu bo-tta-ri

호젓이 걸으면서야 어머니 맘 알았다.

ho-jeo-si geo-leu-myeon-seo-ya

eo-meo-ni mam a-rat-da.

Mother

Bak Byeongsun

Forty Ri of the dawn path which
Snow was falling thick and fast,
Though I shook off so it,
My mother put up a lunch with a wrapper,
On walking along road lonely
I knew her mind at that time.

진달래 연가 (jin-dal-rae yeon-ga)

이 태 극(Lee Taegeuk)

철길 가 흐드러진 함박웃음 밀물로 와
cheol-gil-ga heu-deu-reo-jin
ham-bak u-seum mil-mul-ro wa
연분홍 맺힌 사연 찾아 드는 이 오후는
yeon-bun-hong mae-chin sa-yeon
cha-ja deu-neu i-o-hu-neun
스치는 꽃샘바람도 가슴 깊이 안긴다.
seu-chi-neun kkot-saem-ba-ram-do
ga-seum gi-pi an-gin-da.

The love song of azalea

Lee Taegeuk

A broad-blown peony laugh at the railway side,

Coming on the tide,

This afternoon come to see

Contents be related with pink,

A chill wind

In the flowering season

Is embraced in my deep heart.

* 꽃샘바람: A chill wind in the flowering season(9 syllables:9음절)

사랑 (sa-rang)

이 우 종(Lee Woojong)

살아서 숨쉴 때만 손목을 잡아주고
sa-ra-seo sum-swil ttae-man
son-mo-geul ja-ba ju-go
피어서 있을 때만 꽃이라고 부르지만
pi-eo-seo i-sseul-ttae-man
kko-chi-ra bu-reu-ji-man)
사랑은 무덤에서도 타오르는 불길인 걸.
sarang-eun mu-deom-e-seo-do
ta-o-reu-neun bul-gil-in geol.

Love

Lee Woojong

While she only lives and breathes
He takes her by the hand,

Though he only calls her flower
When she is in beautiful bloom.

Love, it is the fire burning briskly
Even if in a grave.

가을밤 (ga-eul-bam)

정 석 주(Jeong Seokju)

돌아가 돌아가서
do-ra-ga do-ra-ga-seo
가을 창을 손짓하며
ga-eul chang-eul son-ji-ta-myeo

국화잎 몇 낱 끼워
guk-hwa-ip myeon-nat kki-wo
창호지를 발라놓고
chang-ho-ji-reul bal-ra-noko

달빛이 베어들 쯤엔
dal-bichi be-eo-deul jjeu-men
촛불 하나 밝혔으면.
chot-bul-hana bal-kyeo-sseu-myeon.

Fall night

Jeong Seokju

Returning, returning go,
Calling fall window by signs,

Being stuck some chrysanthemums
On the window papers,

About the time when moonlight shines,
I would like to light a candle.

연 · 2 (yeon · 2)

성 효(Seong-hyo)

여기 저기 누구인가? yeo-gi jeo-gi nu-gu-in-ga?
햇불을 들고 선 이는 hwaet-bul deul-go seon i-neun

지나친 겁의 화살 ji-na-chin geo-bui hwa-sal
깨우치는 무상의 빛은 kkae-u-chi-neun

소중한 so-jung-han
찰라의 신비 chalra-ui sinbi
비밀스런 마음의 문. bi-mil-seu-reon ma-eum-ui mun.

The lotus

Seong-hyo

Who are they? here and there,
Those who stand raising the torches,

Excessive Aeon's arrow
Awakes the light of free of charge,

the precious,
The mystery of ksana,
It Is a secret door of mind.

다도茶道 (da-do)

옥 경 국(Ok Gyeongguk)

선비의 붓끝에서 피어나는 난향을 닮아
seon-bi-ui bu-kkeu-te-seo
pi-eo-na-neun nan-hyang-reul dal-ma
여백의 너른 공간 펼쳐진 녹향 따라
yeo-bae-gui neo-reun gong-gan
pyeol-chyeo-jin no-kyang tta-ra
서둘던 구름 한 무리 찻물소리에 귀를 씻네.
seo-dul-deon gu-reum han muri
chan-mul sori-e gwi-reul ssin-ne.

The tea ceremony

Ok Gyeongguk

Taking after perfume of orchid rising
From the point of a scholar' brush,
Following green perfume stretched
At the wide space of a blank space,
A bundle of clouds be in hasten
Washes ears with the voice of tea-water.

불굴가不屈歌 (bul-gul-ga)

변 안 렬(Byeon Anryeol)

가슴에 구멍 뚫어 동아줄로 꿰어 매어

ga-seum-e gu-meong ttu-reo

dong-a jul-ro kkwe-eo mae-eo

앞뒤로 끌고 당겨 이 한 몸 가루된들

ap-dwi-ro kkeul-go dang-gyeo

i-han mom ga-ru-doen-deul)

내님을 빼앗는 일만은 굽힐 줄이 없어라

nae ni-meul ppae-an-neun il-ma-neun

gu-pil-jul-ri eop-seo-ra.

Indomitable poem

Byeon, Anryeol

Making a hole on my breast,
Getting stitches it with rope,
Pulling the rope front and rear,
Though this body becomes the flour,
I will be indomitable to
One thing that thou dislodge my king.

부록

1. 로마자 표기법, 외래어 표기법

로마자 표기법은 우리말을 로마자를 이용해서 적는 것을 가리킨다. 다음에서 찬찬히 살펴보며 익혀보자.

서울seoul, 국민 gungmin

'서울'은 'ㅅ-s, ㅓeo, 우-u, ㄹ-l'로 적은 것이고 'gungmin'은 '국민'의 소리 '궁민'을 'ㄱ-g, ㅜ-u, ㅇ-ng, ㅁ-m, l-i, ㄴ-n'을 적은 것이다.

이에 비해 외래어 표기법은 외국에서 들어온 개념이나 물건의 이름 따위를 우리말로 옮겨 적은 것을 가리킨다.

computer 컴퓨터, coffee shop 커피숍, television 텔레비전… 등이다.

2. 로마자 표기법 규정 익히기 · 1

자모별표기									
모음									
ㅏ	ㅓ	ㅗ	ㅜ	ㅡ	ㅣ	ㅐ	ㅔ	ㅚ	ㅟ
a	eo	o	u	eu	i	ae	e	oe	wi
ㅑ	ㅕ	ㅛ	ㅠ	ㅒ	ㅖ	ㅘ	ㅙ	ㅝ	ㅞ
ya	yeo	yo	yu	yae	ye	wa	wae	wo	w u
자음									
ㄱ	ㄲ	ㅋ	ㄷ	ㄸ	ㅌ	ㅂ	ㅃ	ㅍ	
g, k	kk	k	d,t	tt	t	b, p	pp	p	
ㅈ	ㅉ	ㅊ	ㅅ	ㅆ	ㅎ	ㄴ	ㅁ	ㅇ	ㄹ
j	jj	ch	s	ss	h	n	m	ng	r, l

3. 로마자 표기법 규정 익히기 · 2

1) '신라'는 소리 나는 대로 Silla로 적는다. 현행 로마자 표기법은 우리말의 소리를 적도록 되어 있다. 이는 외국인에게 우리말의 발음을 알려 주기 위한 것이다. '신라'를 Sinla로 적어 놓고 [실라]로 읽기를 기대하는 것은 불가능에 가깝다. 그런 까닭에 '종로'는 Jongno, '독립문'은 Dongnimmun으로 적는다.

2) 널리 알려진 지명도 고쳐야 한다. '제주' Jeju, '부산'은 Busan이 된다. 널리 알려진 지명이라고 예외를 둘 경우에는 어떤 지명은 종전의 표기법대로 적고 어떤 지명은 새 표기 법에 따라야 하는지 판단할 수가 없어서 큰 혼란에 빠질 위험이 있기 때문이다.

3) 학교와 같은 단체명은 종전의 표기법을 그대로 쓸 수 있다. 즉 '건국'은 Konkuk으로 '연세'는 Yonsei로 쓸 수 있으며 '현대'는 Hyundai로 '대우'는 Daewoo로 쓸 수 있다. 그렇지만 지명이 포함되어 있는 '부산대학교', '제주대학교' 등은 모두 지명에 맞춰 로마자 표기를 바꾸어야 한다.

4) 길 이름에 숫자가 들어 있는 경우는 숫자 앞에서 띄어 쓰고 숫자 뒤의 ( )안에 숫자의 우리말 발음을 로마자로 적는다. 예를 들어 '장미1길'은 Jangmi I(il)-gil, '장미2길'은 Jangmi 2(i)-gil로 적는다. '-길' 대신 '-가'를 쓰는 경우도 마찬가지다. '종로1가', '종로2가'는 Jongno 1(il)-ga, Jongno 2(i)-ga로 적는다. 다만 '로(路)'의 경우에는 이와는 달리 붙임표를 넣지 않고 음운 환경에 따라 lo, ro, no 등으로 구분해서 적는다. 예를 들어 '한강1로', '한강2로', '한강3로'는 Hanggang 1(il)lo, Hanggang 2(i)ro, Hanggang 3(sam)no로 적는다.

5) 행정 구역 단위나 지명인 경우에는 전체가 하나의 이름이기 때문에 전체를 소리 나는 대로 적는다. 그러므로 Sinbanpo가 옳다. '북수원', '서대전', '동대구' 등도 Buksuwon, Seodaejeon, Dongdaegu 등으로 적는다.

6) '강서소방서길'은 'Gangseosobangseo-gil'로 적는다. 길 이름을 로마자로 적을 때는 국어의 발음을 로마자로 적는 것이 원칙이다. 다만 다음의 두 가지는 예외이다.

(1) 길 이름에 외래어가 사용된 경우에는 외래어 원어를 밝혀 적는다.

올림픽길 Olympic-gil(O) Olimpik-gil(X)

(2) 학교나 회사에서 쓰는 관습적 표기를 인정하여 기관이나 단체 등의 이름이 길에 붙는 경우 원래의 기관 이름과 일치하도록 적는다.

연세대길 Yonseidae-gil(O) Yeonsedae-gil(X)

따라서 '강서소방서길'을 로마자로 적을 때 'Gangseo Fire Station-gil'처럼 영어 번역어를 쓰지 않고 'Gangseosobangseo-gil'처럼 국어 발음대로 쓴다.

7) '로(路)'는 붙임표를 써서 따로 구분하지 않는다. 즉 '종로'는 Jongno이다. 로마자 표기법에는 행정 구역 단위를 나타내는 '도, 시, 군, 구, 읍, 면, 리, 동'과 '길, 가(街)' 앞에 붙임표를 넣고, 붙임표 앞뒤에서 일어나는 음운 변화는 표기에 반영하지 않도록 규정하고 있다. 예를 들어 '청량리'는 Cheongnyang-ri로 적고 '현북면'은 Hyeonbuk-myeon

으로 적는다. '로'는 이와는 달리 붙임표 없이 소리나는 대로 적는다. 즉 '종로', '통일로', '을지로'는 각각 Jongno, Tongillo, Euliiro로 적는다.

8) '김치'와 '태권도'는 우리나라를 대표하는 문화적 상징물로, Oxford English Dictionary등 일부 영어 사전에 이미 Kimchi, taekwondo로 등재되어 있다.

이것을 예외로 인정하여 그대로 쓰자는 의견이 있었으나 새 표기법에 맞게 gimchi, taegwondo로 쓰는 것이 원칙적으로 옳다.

영어권에서 그들이 써 오던 방식에 따라 kimchi, taegwon으로 쓰는 것은 어쩔 수 없지만, 우리가 홍보물이나 안내 책자를 새롭게 만들 때에는 로마자 표기법에 맞게 gimchi, taegwondo로 써야 한다. 다만 상품의 이름이나 제품명 등으로 이미 사용해 오고 있는 경우에는 kimchi, taekwondo를 계속 쓸 수 있다.

9) '불국사', '화엄사'의 로마자 표기는 Bulguksa, Hwaeomsa 등으로 적는다. '불국사', '화엄사' 전체를 한 단어로 보아 전체를 로마자로 적는다. 마찬가지로 '금강', '속리산' 등도

Geum River, Songni Mt.으로 적지 않고, Geumgang, Songnisan으로 적는다. 다만 외국인들에게 그 명칭이 나타내는 대상이 무엇인지 뜻을 보여 주고자 하는 경우에는 Bulguksa (Temple), Songnisan (Mountain), Deoksugung (Palace)처럼 해당하는 영어 단어를 ( ) 안에 표기한다.

10) '북악'의 로마자 표기 또한 Bukak으로 적기 쉽다. k, t, p로 적는 것은 'ㄱ, ㄷ, ㅂ'이 받침 '글자'일 때가 아니라 받침 '소리'일 때라는 것에 주의해야 한다. '북'이라는 글자에 이끌려서 자칫 '북'이 들어간 말을 모두 Buk로 적기 쉬운데, 로마자 표기는 글자가 아니라 발음에 따라야 함을 잊지 말아야 한다. 똑같은 '북'이라도 '북부'처럼 자음 앞에서는 'ㄱ'이 받침 소리가 되어 Bukbu로 적어야 하지만, '북악'처럼 뒷말이 모음으로 시작할 때는 'ㄱ'받침이 뒤 음절의 첫소리가 되어 [부각]으로 소리가 나므로 Bugak으로 적는다.

마찬가지로 'ㄱ' 받침 뒤에 'ㄴ'이나 'ㅁ' 소리가 오면 'ㄱ' 소리가 'ㅇ' 소리로 바뀌므로 그때에는 ng로 적는다. 따라서 '북문'은 [붕문]으로 소리나므로 Bukmun이 아니라 Bungmun으로 적는다.

11) 낙동강'은 [낙똥강]으로 소리 나더라도 Nakdonggang 으로 적는다. 우리말의 된소리되기 현상은 음운 환경에 따라 예측 가능하지 않은 경우가 많이 있다. 예를 들어 '물고기'와 '불고기'의 '고기'는 똑같이 'ㄹ' 소리 다음에 있지만 [물꼬기]에서는 된소리가 되나 [불고기]에서는 되지 않는다. 이러한 이유로 어떤 경우에 된소리가 나는지 결정하기 어려운 경우가 많아 표기하지 않기로 한 것이다.

된소리되기를 표기에 반영하지 않은 경우, [낙똥강]과 [물꼬기]를 외국인들이 [낙동강], [물고기]로 부자연스럽게 발음할 가능성이 있지만 이것을 우리가 '낙동강', '물고기'로 알아듣기에는 어려움이 없을 것이다.

'팔당, 일산' 등도 발음이 분명히 [팔땅], [일싼]으로 나지만 된소리 발음을 무시하고 Paldang, Ilsan으로 적는다. 또 '당고개'도 발음에 관계없이 Danggogae로 적는 것이 맞다.

12) '낚시'의 받침 'ㄲ'은 'ㄱ'으로 발음 되므로 kk가 아닌 k로 적는다. 즉 '낚시'는 [낙씨]로 발음되므로 naksi로 적어야한다. 다만 된소리되기는 표기에 반영하지 않는다는 규정 때문에 [낙씨]를 nakssi로 적지 않고 naksi로 적는다.

13) 사람 이름을 적을 때에는 우리말 어순에 따라 성을 앞에, 이름을 뒤에 적는다. 성과 이름 사이에는 반점(,)을 찍는 경우도 있고, 찍지 않고 띄어쓰기만 하는 경우도 있다. 요즈음은 후자가 우세하다. 또한 이름은 음절과 음절 사이를 붙여 쓰며, 음절을 반드시 구분하고자 하는 경우에는 그 사이에 붙임표를 넣을 수 있다.

예를 들어 '홍길동'이란 이름은 Hong Gildong 또는 Hong Gil-dong로 쓴다. 성을 이름 뒤에 적는 방식(Gildong Hong)은 물론, 이름의 각 음절 사이를 띄어 쓰거나(Hong Gil dong), 이름의 두 번째 음절 첫 자를 대문자로 쓰는 방식(Hong GilDong)은 옳지 않다.

Hong Gildong(원칙)
Hong Gil-dong(허용)
Hong, Gildong(허용)
Gil Dong Hong (×)

또한 이름의 음절 사이에서 일어나는 음운 변화는 표기에 반영하지 않고 글자대로 쓴다. 예를 들어 '한복남'이라는 이름은 [한봉남]으로 소리 나지만, 발음에 따라 Han Bongnam(또는 Han Bong-nam)으로 적지 않고 철자에 따라 Han Boknam(또는 Han Bok-nam)으로 적는다. 이것은 한자(漢字)로 된 이름뿐만 아니라 고유어 이름도 마찬가지여서, '빛나'도 Binna가 아니라 Bitna(또는 Bit-na)로 적는다. 우리나라 사람들의 이름은 대개 한 자 한 자마다 의미가 있고, 특히 항렬을 따르는 경우가 많아서 각 음절별로 음가를 살려 적도록 한 것이다.♣

* Author profile

* Poetess, Korean Literature, Ph.D. English literature, B.A
* Collected Sijo Poetry : 『A train journey』, 『A scent of
  Sijo』 besides, a work in six volumes.
* Free Poems : 『The scape of mind』 besides, a work in
  two volumes.
* Learned books : 『Modern Sijo, A way of the proper form』
  a work in fifteen volumes. 『Understanding of literature』
  (The year 2012, The Culture Ministry Selected as one of
  the outstanding academic books).
* Sijo Literature Work Awardee (2006).
* Gosan, Yun, Seondo Sijo Literature Awardee (2012).
* Han, Haun, Literature Awardee(2013, literary criticism).

* Korean Sijo Writers's Association's Central Committee.
* Korean Modern Poet Association, Central Committee.
* Korean Sijo-Sarang Writers's Association, Vice-chairman.
* Ewha University Alumni the Literary Association's a director.
* Corporation, The Society for Sijo Literary Promotion. The chief director (2011~2013), A adviser.

이정자의 영역시조(1)

빗방울 A raindrop

| 초판 1쇄 인쇄일 | | 2015년 9월 9일 |
| 초판 1쇄 발행일 | | 2015년 9월 10일 |

엮은이		이정자
펴낸이		정구형
편집장		김효은
편집/디자인		김진솔 우정민 박재원
마케팅		정찬용 정진이
영업관리		한선희 이선건 최재영
책임편집		김진솔
인쇄처		덕성문화사
펴낸곳		국학자료원 새미(주)

등록일 2005 03 15 제25100-2005-000008호
서울특별시 강동구 성안로 13 (성내동, 현영빌딩 2층)
Tel 442-4623 Fax 6499-3082
www.kookhak.co.kr
kookhak2001@hanmail.net

| ISBN | | 979-11-86478-41-7 *03800 |
| 가격 | | 12,000원 |